Flea Biscuit's Summer Vacation

Matthew Bonazzoli

For everyone who works to rescue our furry friends.

CONTENTS

Acknowledgements

Thank you to my sister Laura for editing, to Jim Odo for the illustrations and to everyone who bought the first book and encouraged me to continue with the characters.

Chapter 1

Brush Before Bedtime

The little girl slowly rolled the brush from Flea Biscuit's head, over the red collar on his neck, and down his back to his tail. Every now and then, when he was certain the bristles had done their work, he changed position, then closed his eyes again and purred. She brushed him every night when they finished playing and it was almost bedtime. It always made him sleepy.

Flea Biscuit began to yawn. "This is my favorite time," he thought. "It is getting dark outside, the girl is finished with her chores, and the house is quiet." Then again, he loved curling up on the blankets beside the girl as she slept, and he also loved the smile she would give him when he gently tapped her cheek to let her know that it was time to wake up. One thing Flea Biscuit knew for certain was that the girl and her mother loved him. That made him happy, and he would always try his best to make them happy as well.

When the little girl finished brushing him, he stretched out on the bed. "Time for sleep," he thought. However, instead of getting under the blankets to go to bed, the girl went to the closet and brought out the small plastic carrier they had used to bring him to the doctor. He didn't like going to the doctor, even though he knew it was necessary to keep him healthy and fit, so he dove under a pillow. When the girl didn't try to catch him, he peeked out. She had gone back to her closet and was pulling out her suitcase. She placed it on the bed near him and began to pack some clothes in it.

"What's this?" thought the little tiger. "Perhaps I'm not going to the doctor and we are all going on a fun adventure!" He began to get very excited and, while the girl packed her things, he crawled into her suitcase so she would be sure to bring him along.

The girl laughed and gently lifted him off her clothes and placed him back on the bed. Flea Biscuit waited for just the right moment and climbed right back in on top of her neatly packed clothes. The girl waved her finger at him and giggled. He loved to make her smile and gave her a long, slow blink in return.

She again lifted him out of the suitcase and placed him on the bed. This time Flea Biscuit pretended to lose interest, but as soon as the girl turned her back, he hopped back in and made himself comfortable again.

When the girl turned and saw him in the suitcase again, she gave him a stern look and slowly closed the lid, leaving Flea Biscuit in the dark. When he heard the zipper moving across the cover, he let out a howl and fought to get out.

The girl quickly unzipped the case. Out he popped. The girl petted him, and he understood that she had just been playing a trick on him. He had learned his lesson. He decided to be content with sitting on the bed, watching her pack, and dreaming about his next adventure.

Chapter 2

A Wet Nose Knows

The sun beat down on the big old house. A warm wind caused the porch swing where Spike was sleeping to sway. Feeling the ruffle through his black fur, he slowly raised his head and opened his eyes. "It is hot today," he thought. "Too hot to hunt." He let out a yawn. "Perhaps tonight."

Cheeto was dozing beneath the porch swing. Upon hearing the yawn, he opened one eye and looked up to see if Spike had decided to move. "Is it lunch time?" he asked. When he saw Spike lower his head back down, he too went back to sleep.

Suddenly, a loud shot sounded from the edge of the forest. In a flash, Spike and Cheeto were both standing and alert. "Someone is hunting?" Cheeto asked.

"Yes," replied Spike. "But why so close to the house?"

The front door to the big old house swung open and the man quickly came outside. With a sigh of relief, he saw his two cats safely on the porch. He was scanning the forest, looking for a sign of the hunter, when a large, golden brown dog came bounding out of the woods and onto the grass. She was soon followed by an old farmer carrying a rifle over his shoulder.

The farmer waved in the direction of the big old house as his dog ran left and right exploring the front yard. The man stepped off the porch to meet him, but closed the wooden gate behind him.

"Why do you suppose he did that?" asked Cheeto. "We can easily jump over the railing, or squeeze through the posts, for that matter."

Spike stretched and looked at Cheeto. "I don't think he was trying to keep us in," he replied. "He wants to keep the dog away from us."

"Well, surely I won't go near a dog," said Cheeto. "Especially not after the nasty bite I got last winter. Dogs are stupid and dangerous."

"No, we're not!" A wet nose suddenly poked between the railings. Cheeto jumped up onto the porch swing and Spike arched his back and fluffed out his fur.

"It speaks!" proclaimed Cheeto.

"Be gone, wolf!" hissed Spike as he darted toward the railing waving his claws.

"I'm a retriever dog, not a wolf!" The dog spoke quickly and excitedly. "My name is Abigail, but my friends call me Abby. What are your names? Cats do have names, don't they?"

Abby's jovial enthusiasm made Cheeto feel a little less frightened. He looked nervously at the scar on his paw from where he had been bitten. He then decided to answer. "I am called Cheeto," he said, "and this is Spike."

"I said be gone!" shouted Spike, and he leapt forward and swatted at Abby's nose.

Abby jumped back. "My, you certainly aren't very friendly. I guess what they say about cats is true. You are mean and hateful.

"My master and I live on the farm down the road and we are out hunting for the coyotes that have been raiding the local farms and killing chickens… and cats! They kill cats, don't you know?" Abby looked directly at Spike.

"As would you, and all wolves if you got the chance," said Spike harshly.

Abby ignored him. "We almost got one today, but they are very quick. A trio of them has been spotted nearby and they are very dangerous, so please try to stay safe."

"Safe, so you can eat us later?" asked Cheeto timidly. Spike glared at him, angry that he was showing fear.

"Oh, no," said Abby. "I would never eat a cat. We can be friends. Would you like to play with me? I'm very good at chase and tag."

"No!" said Spike. "Don't you have something better to do?"

"Not at the moment," said Abby. She stuck her nose through the railing a second time. She was trying to catch the scent of the two cats so she could remember them.

Spike instinctively swatted her nose again. "Stay away from this house!" he growled.

"You're very mean," said Abby. "Does your master know how mean you are?"

"We don't have a master," said Spike. "We help the man and he helps us."

"I help my master," Abby responded, "and he helps me. I don't see a difference."

"Your master commands you," said Spike, "and he makes you do tricks. We do not do tricks for the man. We work."

Abby looked sad. "I do things that please my master. I like to make him happy because we are a team and he does a lot for me."

"It's not the same," said Cheeto, "but I don't expect a wolf to understand."

"Stop calling me a wolf," growled Abby. "I am a dog and proud to be. You keep reminding me why some people do not like cats. Everyone likes dogs." Abby began to hop around happily at the thought.

"My man does not have a dog," said Spike.

Abby stopped bouncing and looked at the two cats. "That's because you are mean and a dog wouldn't like you."

Spike hissed, again showing his claws.

Abby backed away. With a look of disappointment in her eyes, she turned to leave. "I never had a cat for a friend, and I guess I never will," she said.

Her master whistled to her. She trotted off, acting as if what Spike and Cheeto had said didn't bother her. "Cats are terrible at chase and tag anyway," she told herself. "They only care about themselves." Still, she was sad that they couldn't be friends just because they were different.

The old farmer led Abby back into the woods and the man headed back toward the house.

"Well, that was something, wasn't it?" said Cheeto. "I've never spoken to a dog before. I never even knew they could speak. Have you, Spike? Ever spoken to a dog, I mean."

"No," said Spike. "I do not like wolves. Their wet noses and following their humans around like conspiring servants. Wolves are not to be trusted, friendly or not."

Cheeto hopped off the porch swing. "Yes, dogs are the same as wolves to me, too," he agreed. "Not a difference in the world."

Spike jumped back onto the porch swing, looked down at Cheeto, and hissed. "And the same as coyotes."

Cheeto watched Abby and the old farmer disappear into the woods. Then he asked Spike, "Are we mean?"

Spike just muttered, "It's hot." He closed his eyes and put his head down.

Cheeto lay down and wanted to go back to sleep, but he could not forget how he had behaved toward Abby. "I have never been one to withhold friendship," he thought. "Still, she is a dog and dogs are not to be trusted." Something about this thought bothered him, though. He tried to think of reasons why cats and dogs could not be friends, until finally he decided that it was too hot to think today. He closed his eyes. When they heard the man coming up the porch steps, Cheeto and Spike looked up. The man gave them a look of concern as he passed.

Chapter 3

Cats and Bats

Spike paced by the front door. "It's a perfect night for hunting and I want out!" he howled. Each time he caught the man's attention, he would swat at the door.

Cheeto sat calmly by, somewhat amused.

"Out!" hissed Spike. He walked up to the man and swatted at his leg. "Out! Let me out!"

The man was sitting in his chair reading in front of a whirring fan. He looked down at Spike sympathetically, but he did not let him outside.

Spike went back to the door and swatted at it. "Let me out!" he hissed again.

"He's not listening to you, Spike," Cheeto finally said.

"I can see that!" Now Spike turned and swatted at Cheeto.

Cheeto hopped just out of range and sat back down. "I think he's worried about the coyotes."

"I'm not afraid of coyotes, wolves, or any other beast of the forest," hissed Spike.

"I think the man knows this, Spike," said Cheeto, "and that is why he is afraid for you. He doesn't want either of us to come to any harm, so he is keeping us in tonight. I am grateful to have a man who looks out for me and wants me to be safe."

Spike let out another roar and continued swatting at the door.

"It is a nice night," Cheeto said. "Maybe we can slip through the window in the attic and go out on the rooftop. You enjoy watching the bats clear the yard of insects."

Spike shot an angry look toward Cheeto. "That will only remind me that they are free to hunt and I am being kept a prisoner here!"

Cheeto attempted to ease Spike's anger. "Come now, you've been out hunting all week. Why don't you take a night off and relax a little?"

"I don't want to relax! I want to hunt!" Spike shouted, hitting the door with each word.

"If that's how you feel, fine," said Cheeto with a hint of mischief in his voice. "You just stay here all night and swat at the door. I'm going up to the roof to enjoy the night air."

Spike looked back at the man, who was now ignoring him completely. He then watched Cheeto hop up the stairs. "Fine!" he groaned, and followed his friend up to the roof.

Spike and Cheeto settled down at the edge of the roof overlooking the front yard. For a long time, Spike stared upward silently, his head bobbing along with the flight of the passing bats. He was trying to imagine himself soaring through the air hunting with them. He began to mimic the bat's high clicking sounds as if he was calling to one.

"What did you say?" asked Cheeto whimsically.

Spike snapped out of his dream. "Nothing!" he said, embarrassed that he had made the sounds.

Suddenly the yard below them brightened with the headlights of an approaching car. "We've got a visitor," said Cheeto. The two cats watched as the car parked and a woman and a little girl got out. They were carrying something.

"This could be my chance to get outside!" said Spike as he hurried back to the attic window.

"It's Flea Biscuit's humans!" shouted Cheeto, following right behind.

Chapter 4

Wolves and Wails and Puppy Dog Tails

The little girl handed the cat carrier to the man, then turned and followed her mother back to the car. Like a streak of lightning, Spike ran for the door, but just before he reached it, the man closed it tight. Spike almost ran into it. "No!" he howled in frustration.

The man placed the cat carrier on the floor and opened the little door. As Flea Biscuit hopped out, the bell on his collar made a soft chime.

Stepping down the last few stairs, Cheeto let out a loud, "Hello, Little One!"

"Tom, I'm so happy to see you!" Flea Biscuit walked up to Cheeto and rubbed his cheeks against him. "It is good to be back."

"The man has named me," Cheeto said proudly. "You can now call me Cheeto."

Flea Biscuit stood straight and raised one paw. "Well, Cheeto it is, Sir." They began to laugh.

"That is a lovely red collar you have around your neck," said Cheeto.

"Thank you," responded Flea Biscuit. "My humans gave it to me. I feel like a prince! And listen. When I walk, it jingles!" The little tiger happily paraded in a circle to demonstrate.

17

"Your highness!" exclaimed Cheeto.

Spike interrupted their happy reunion. "Are your humans returning you because they've discovered that you can't hunt? We don't have room for a third cat here!"

"I'm just here for my summer vacation!" said Flea Biscuit excitedly.

"Did you see his lovely collar, Spike?" asked Cheeto.

Spike closely examined the bright red collar with the bell on it. Then he snickered. "The man tried to put a collar on me once."

"What happened?" asked Flea Biscuit.

"I made certain that he never tried to put one on me again!"

Cheeto stood on his back legs and imitated Spike waving his claws around. "Don't mind Spike," he said as Flea Biscuit giggled. "As you can see, he hasn't changed much. So you'll be staying with us for a few days then?"

"Yes! We'll have so much fun," said Flea Biscuit.

Spike rolled his eyes and walked away. "Oh, this is too much to bear," he moaned. "Please let me outside!"

Flea Biscuit turned to Cheeto. "So, you are allowed to live in the house now?" he asked.

"Yes," answered Cheeto. "I live here with Spike and the man. I help Spike with the hunting. He pretends that he doesn't want me here, but that's just his way. We are friends now. You see, in the spring I was bitten by a coyote, and Spike brought me to the man, who helped me get well and gave me a name. I knew I was part of the household then."

18

"What's a ky—ky—?" Flea Biscuit struggled to repeat the word *coyote*, but couldn't get it right.

"Another word for a dog or a wolf," said Cheeto.

"A wolf bit you?" asked Flea Biscuit. His eyes darted nervously left and right.

"Yes," said Cheeto with anger in his voice. He squinted as he looked directly at the little tiger. "Dogs, wolves, coyotes. They're all the same. Canines, they're called. Vicious and spiteful. Always out to kill and eat a cat if they get the chance."

As Cheeto told the story of his encounter, Flea Biscuit was filled with awe and fear. He had never encountered a wolf and hoped that he never did. He began to hate all canines just because of the story Cheeto was telling him.

"In fact," said Cheeto, "that's why we're not allowed outside tonight. A pack of these coyote killers has been roaming out in the woods nearby and the man doesn't want us to be eaten!" Realizing that he was scaring his friend a little too much, Cheeto made a barking sound and pretended to chase after Flea Biscuit, who ran laughing down the hallway—until he got to the kitchen and ran headlong into Spike.

Spike raised a paw to swat at Flea Biscuit. "Be gone, Flea!" he shouted. "I have no patience for your nonsense tonight."

"Ah, leave the little one alone, Spike," said Cheeto. "It's good to have us all together for a few days, isn't it?"

Spike simply grunted and walked away. His long claws clicked on the floor as he went.

Chapter 5

The Scaredy Cat

After breakfast the next morning, Spike decided to wait by the door, hoping the man would finally let him out.

In the kitchen, Flea Biscuit and Cheeto had just finished eating. The little tiger turned to his friend and excitedly asked, "What shall we do today? My humans do not allow me to go outside, so I will need to stay in the house."

"Well," said Cheeto, "there is much of this house that we can explore. Then we can take a nap. When we wake up, we can have lunch and go to one of the windows and look at the birds. Then we can take another nap, and then it will be dinner time."

"That sounds like a perfect day," said Flea Biscuit.

Cheeto led him to the large staircase by the door. The man had just gone outside to speak with the old farmer and had latched the screen door behind him. Spike was ramming his head into the base of the door, trying to get it open.

"Relax, Spike," advised Cheeto. "Don't hurt yourself. You'll be able to go outside soon."

"No!" hissed Spike as he continued his work. "I will not be held prisoner by anyone. With each hit, the latch bounced up and down and the door seemed to swing a little further open. Cheeto began to hop upstairs, but Flea Biscuit paused to watch Spike work. Suddenly the latch on the door popped and the door opened a few inches. Spike was just about to squeeze through the opening when suddenly Abby's nose came poking through from outside.

Abby looked right at Flea Biscuit. "Want to play?" she asked, and pushed her way into the house.

"Wolf!" shouted Flea Biscuit in a panic. He turned and ran down the hall, his little bell ringing as he went.

"Oh, chase!" Abby said excitedly. She ran to catch the little cat. "I'm very good at playing chase."

Flea Biscuit ran around the corner and into the kitchen, his back feet slipping across the floor. "Wolf! Wolf!" he cried.

Spike and Cheeto ran after Abby, shouting at her to stop, but she was having so much fun playing her game, she didn't hear them.

The little tiger cat ran up the back stairs, across the hall, and down the main stairway screaming, "Wolf! Wolf!"

Abby wasn't far behind.

Bang! Flea Biscuit's head slammed into the screen door. It swung open and he tumbled outside. Then the door slammed shut behind him, and the latch closed again. Eagerly, Abby pawed the door, wanting to continue the chase, but the latch remained fastened. Now she was trapped in the house, too. As Abby, Cheeto, and Spike looked out through the screen, they saw Flea Biscuit running toward the man and the farmer. The man reached down to try to grab Flea Biscuit, but the little cat ran past him into the woods, howling in terror.

"Come back, little one!" shouted Cheeto.

Spike turned to Abby. He was furious. "How dare you enter this house!" he spat. He rose on his hind legs and swatted her on the nose.

Abby looked puzzled. "Your friend is very good at chase," she said. "I would have caught him, though, if the door hadn't closed. I'm very good at chase, too."

"He wasn't playing!" cried Cheeto. "Couldn't you see he was scared of you? Now he's run into the woods, where he'll get lost. This is all your fault, you stupid wolf!"

Abby lowered her head and let out a whimper.

Cheeto immediately felt sorry for his outburst. He apologized.

"It's all right," she said sadly. "I am not a wolf, but I am sorry. I thought he was playing."

"A lot of good sorry will do him," said Spike as he tapped his claws on the floor.

"We'll have to go and find him," said Cheeto.

Spike sighed. "Must we?"

"Yes!" said Cheeto angrily.

Abby barked enthusiastically. "I will help you! I'm very good at tracking. I can use my nose to follow his trail."

"And why should we trust you, wolf?" said Spike suspiciously. "You were just chasing him."

"Because," Abby answered, "as I keep telling you, I am not a wolf. I am a dog and my master and your man are friends and maybe we can be friends, too."

Cheeto thought for a moment. It was true that people were friends to both dogs and cats, so why couldn't dogs and cats be friends? Maybe Abby was right. After a moment, he agreed. "Well, lassie, I never turn down a new friendship, if that's your aim. We will find him together."

Spike looked at the latch on the door. "It's no use trying to get outside now. When the man comes back and opens the door, we'll try to escape."

"What about the coyotes?" asked Cheeto.

"We will need to be careful," said Abby, "but if we do cross paths, I will protect you."

"Worry about yourself!" said Spike. "Cats can climb trees far beyond the reach of any coyote. Or dog."

Just then, the man began to open the door to let Abby go to her master. As soon as he unhooked the latch, the dog and the two cats pushed the door hard and ran toward the woods. The man and the old farmer called after them, but they kept going until they had disappeared in the brush at the edge of the tree line.

After arriving near where Flea Biscuit had entered the forest, Abby put her nose to the ground and began to sniff for signs of the trail. "Hopefully he hasn't gone too far," said Cheeto.

"If he's smart," said Spike, "which he isn't, he'll stop to wait for us to find him."

"I've got his trail," said Abby. "This way!"

Chapter 6

Trails and Tribulations

Flea Biscuit ran left and right, around trees and rocks, deeper and deeper into the woods. It was only when he was too tired to go any further that he realized he was no longer being chased. He sat down to rest and look around, but could not figure out which direction he had come from. He had outrun his pursuer, but had not paid attention to where he was running. "Uh, oh," he thought anxiously. "I'm not supposed to be outside." Once he had caught his breath, he noticed an overgrown path through the woods. Maybe it led back to the big house! He wandered off through the leaves.

The trees in the forest were lush and green and beautiful, he thought. However, the leaves and ferns made it difficult for the little cat to see more than a short distance in front of him. "This all looks so different from when I was here in the winter," he recalled. "I got lost then, too. I wish Cheeto were here to tell me which way to go."

Soon the overgrown path ended in a cluster of stones. He hopped up onto one of them and looked about. Everything looked the same to him. In each direction were trees, ferns, rocks, and more trees. He thought he would let out a howl to see if it would be answered, but then he remembered that Cheeto had warned him that a pack of dangerous coyotes might be nearby. He did not want to become their dinner. "Well, this direction is as good as any," he thought, and headed deeper into the forest. The longer he wandered, however, the more confused he became. He was not skilled in the old ways of the field cats and did not know how to mark his trails to help him find his way. "I know I saw that tree before," he thought. "Or was it this tree?"

Meanwhile, some distance away, Spike, Cheeto, and Abby continued their search. The two cats were aware that Abby's nose was leading them into unfamiliar territory. Spike was worried that soon they might very well be lost, too. The idea of relying on Abby to find the way back was not appealing to him at all.

Suddenly, Abby stopped, raised her head, and sniffed the air. "We are being followed," she said.

"How do you know?" asked Cheeto.

"I can smell the coyotes that my master and I were hunting yesterday. They are pacing behind us at a safe distance, trying to avoid being discovered."

"Likely they are waiting for us to tire or sleep," Spike said. He turned to Abby. "Two cats would be a good meal for them, and maybe you would join in the feast?"

Abby looked offended. "I told you I would never eat a cat."

Cheeto brushed up against Abby. "I believe you," he said.

Abby licked Cheeto's head.

Spike turned back toward the path. "Well," he muttered, "we may get our chance to find out soon enough."

Chapter 7

Possum Stew

Flea Biscuit wandered down another of the many overgrown paths in the woods, his bell jingling softly as he went.

Deep within his den, an old possum was having his lunch when he heard the sound of the little cat's bell. Intrigued, he poked his head out of his den just as Flea Biscuit approached.

"Why, hello there!" said the little tiger.

The possum looked at the silver bell and then at Flea Biscuit.

"I'm trying to find my way back home," said Flea Biscuit. "I came from the big old house. My friends are Cheeto and Spike. Perhaps you know them?"

The possum remained focused on the little cat, but was still and silent, occasionally chewing.

Flea Biscuit wondered if the possum hadn't heard him. He tried again. "I am lost. Can you help me find my way back to the house?"

Still, the old possum just looked at him. Flea Biscuit looked around impatiently. He could see a lake in the distance, and he was thirsty. He shrugged and scampered off.

A moment after Flea Biscuit had started for the lake, the old possum straightened, turned, and pointed in the direction of the big old house. Alas, Flea Biscuit had already gone too far to notice that he was heading further in the wrong direction.

Chapter 8

In a Scent Lost

"I'm losing his scent," said Abby. "We've crossed this spot before, so he's wandering in circles and I'm not sure which way to go now."

"Perhaps we should stop to rest a little while," said Cheeto. "Maybe after a break you'll be able to find where he went."

While Cheeto and Abby sat down to rest, Spike climbed a tree to take a look around and try to listen for the sound of Flea Biscuit's little bell. He was only a few feet off the ground when he noticed three figures coming quickly toward them. The coyotes!

He called out a warning. Instinctively, he and Cheeto climbed high into the tree. Abby stood below and tried to look fierce. She wished her master were there to help.

As the coyotes approached, the largest and leader of the pack hissed at her. "Dog!" he spat, in an old language still familiar to all canines.

"Dog," the second coyote echoed with a similarly insulting tone. The third simply laughed and looked about nervously.

Abby understood the venom in the coyotes' insults, but stood her ground, growling and showing her teeth.

Beneath the tree, the coyotes began circling around Abby, speaking as one. "Hungry. Cat. Hungry." They all yipped and began to howl.

Spike and Cheeto puffed out their fur and tried to look fierce. "Spike," whispered Cheeto. "I think that's the big one who bit me last spring."

"You won't be getting these cats," said Abby in the old canine language. "Not unless you can climb trees."

The three coyotes looked high up into the tree at Spike and Cheeto. "Food," said one slowly. "Hungry," said another. Then the leader glared at Abby and repeated, slowly and menacingly, "Dog!"

Cheeto and Spike couldn't understand the canine words, but they knew the coyote was threatening their companion. Showing their teeth and claws, they began to howl as viciously as they could.

Their outburst—and the size of Spike's claws—frightened the leader of the pack, but he gathered his nerve and hunched down as if ready to attack. Peering at Abby with red eyes, he hissed again. "Dog!"

The other two coyotes, however, seemed frozen in place, staring up at the two howling cats.

This gave Abby a chance to escape. She looked left and right. Then, in a flash, she ran as fast as she could into the woods. The three coyotes leapt after her.

Abby ran through the trees and up a hill. Then she began to make a wide circle. "I am very good at playing chase and tag," she thought. "Better than they will ever be." With each step, she was outpacing the coyotes. She hoped that soon they would tire of the chase and seek easier game to hunt.

Up on the high tree branch, Spike and Cheeto watched as Abby and the coyotes disappeared into the forest.

"What mangy creatures!" said Cheeto. "Filthy and savage!"

Spike shot Cheeto an angry glance. "Have you lived in the man's house so long that you have forgotten what it's like to be desperate and hungry in the wild?"

Cheeto began to respond, but Spike interrupted.

"Be thankful for your comforts," he said, "and never look down upon those less fortunate. Now, let's continue with our search. Just be very careful and stay where there are trees to climb."

The two crawled down from their perch. "I hope Abby will be all right," said Cheeto. "Do you trust her now?"

Spike said nothing except to command, "This way."

He headed off down an overgrown path that looked to Cheeto the same as all the others. "What's down there, Spike?" he asked.

"I have a friend who lives nearby. Maybe he's seen the house cat. If I can locate his den, he may be able to help."

After several minutes of walking, the cats were startled by the sound of something crashing through the leaves and branches. As they leapt up the nearest tree, Abby came bounding out of the woods. "Abby!" cried Cheeto, jumping back to the ground. "You nearly scared me to death."

Abby was panting hard. "I was able to outrun those coyotes and catch your sent. They are not as good at chase as I am. I am very good at chase. I caught your scent and found you. Where are you going?"

Cheeto was surprised and fascinated that Abby had located them by their scent so quickly. "You smelled us from way over the hill?" he asked.

"Well," said Abby, "if a dog is going to be good at chase, she has to learn how to track. I am very good at chase."

Spike did not like the idea that Abby could track him so easily. He made a mental note to groom himself better from now on.

"Where are we going?" repeated Abby.

"There," Spike replied. He descended the tree and crossed the path to a deep den. Slowly, he crawled inside. In a moment, he came back out, followed by a squeaking grey possum.

"He has seen Flea Biscuit," said Spike.

"Do you know where he went?" asked Cheeto. The possum simply looked ahead and remained still.

Abby looked on, bewildered. "That wild beast doesn't understand you," she said. "It's just a forest animal."

"Be quiet," said Spike. "It's true he speaks the old language of the wilderness, but he does understand me."

Abby cautiously approached the possum and took in a few deep breaths of his scent. Cheeto explained to her that

41

domesticated animals like cats and dogs have mostly forgotten the ancient tongue of the forest. However, since he and Spike had once been wild, they had learned. Still, it could take a long time for them to be understood.

After several more minutes of silence, the possum pointed to the large lake where Flea Biscuit had recently headed.

"Thank you," said Spike. He then warned the possum of the nearby coyotes. The possum seemed to shrug.

"Yes," added Cheeto, "they are dangerous and you need to be careful, friend." He slowly blinked toward the possum.

The possum looked at Cheeto, made a squeaking sound, and then crawled back into his den to sleep for the rest of the hot afternoon.

As they walked off toward the lake, Cheeto asked Spike, "How do you know that possum?"

Spike answered with a sly smile. "For the last few years he has come to the porch of the old house on cold nights to eat food the man has left out. I sit by him to be sure he is not disturbed while he eats."

Cheeto suddenly stopped in his tracks. "You used to let the possum eat my food when I was living in the woods?" He sounded indignant.

"Yes, the man left food out for more beasts than you. Besides, now that he has shown us the way to Flea Biscuit, aren't you grateful that I let him have some of your food?"

Abby was amused at Spike's distracting answer.

"Well, sort of," said Cheeto. "I suppose I need to be, but we will talk again of this later."

"We will not," said Spike.

Cheeto let out a huff, but Abby licked his cheek to let him know it was all right. She then put her nose to the ground to follow Flea Biscuit's trail.

Chapter 9

The Tree on the Hill

After Flea Biscuit had a long drink of water from the lake he headed off in search of the big old house again.

He roamed in one direction, then another, but still, nothing looked familiar. Then he spied a large rock. He climbed to the top, his bell chiming with each hop. Through a break in the forest, he could see a field of tall grass in the distance and a hill with an old oak tree on the peak. "If I could climb that tree, I might be able to see where the house is," he thought. He was becoming tired, but he climbed back down and continued walking.

Just as he headed into the field, he heard a rustling noise. He looked back and saw three coyotes coming out of the forest. "Wolves!" he thought. He ducked low to the ground and remained still. He would be safe high in the branches, but the oak tree seemed far away. The coyotes spread out and sniffed the ground as if searching for something. Were they searching for him? As if to answer his question, he heard one of them call out to the others. The word was strange. He wondered if it was "Cat!"

Flea Biscuit ducked further into the tall grass surrounding the hill. Behind him, he could hear the coyotes scampering about and howling for him. They sounded hungry. His heart was racing and he was beginning to panic. The life he had with the little girl flashed before his eyes. She would be so sad if he never made it home again. His love for her gave him a new strength. He was determined to survive. He looked at the top of the hill and fixed his gaze on the tall oak tree. If he could climb high into its branches, he would be safe. Gathering his courage, he sprinted for the tree.

As he ran, the chiming of the bell on his collar alerted the coyotes to exactly where he had been hiding. They headed straight after him.

Flea Biscuit sped through the grass. He kept his eyes trained on the tree's wide branches even as he heard the three hungry coyotes closing in behind him. As he reached the base of the tree, he jumped for the closest branch just as the jaws of his hungry pursuers snapped at his tail.

Back in the forest, the searchers were tired and losing faith that they would ever locate their friend. "We've been to the lake," said Abby, "and I haven't caught a strong scent in a long time. I wonder if that old possum even pointed us in the right direction. Maybe your little friend has wandered in a circle again."

Spike said nothing and just kept walking.

"Come, Abby," said Cheeto. "We can't give up."

Abby looked at Cheeto with new respect. She'd always been told that cats were ignorant, solitary creatures who cared for nothing but themselves. And yet, here they were, out in a dangerous forest searching for one they called their friend.

"That tree high on the hill over yonder," said Cheeto. "Do you see it?"

"Yes," said Spike.

"What about it?" asked Abby.

Spike showed his claws and answered, "We cats can climb high atop those branches and from there we'll be able to scan this entire area for the housecat."

"Aye," added Cheeto, "and if we spot him, we can call him there."

"Good idea." Abby put her nose down to continue searching for a scent. "If he's nearby, I'll find him."

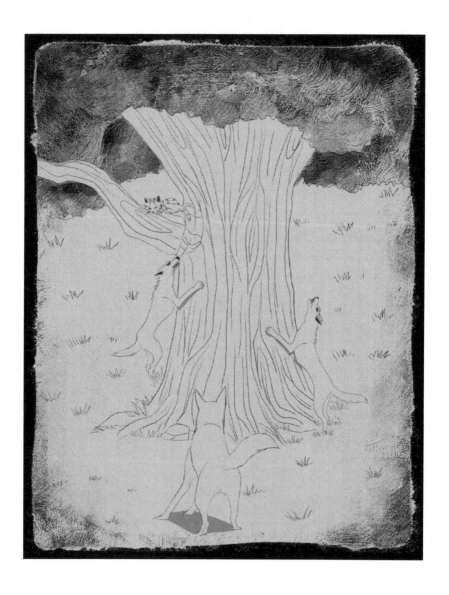

Chapter 10

Catch a Tiger by the Tail

There was a mixture of unsettling scents on the wind as they walked in the direction of the tree on the hill. Abby thought she could smell a cat, but she was also picking up the scent of something more menacing. Suddenly, from the direction of the hill, they heard a cat howling in fear.

"It's Flea Biscuit!" yelled Cheeto.

In the distance, the trio could see the large oak tree and, huddled on one of its lowest branches, the little tiger cat. At the foot of the tree, the three coyotes were jumping at the limb he was clinging to.

"Wolf! Wolf!" cried Flea Biscuit. "Go away!" The coyotes did not go away. Instead, the kitten's cries seemed to make them want him even more. He knew the branch he clung to was not high enough, but he was too frightened to move. Beneath him, the coyotes leapt and nipped, coming closer and closer to his puffed-out fur.

"We've got to do something!" cried Cheeto.

"Even with Abby, we're no match for three wild and hungry coyotes," said Spike. "To try to reach Flea will not go well for any of us."

"I will try to chase them off," Abby said. "They want an easy meal, not a fight, and perhaps if they are challenged, they will back down."

"But they weren't afraid of you before. What if they don't leave?" whimpered Cheeto.

"Then they will fight," interrupted Spike, "and at three to one, I doubt they'll give up so easily."

"Nevertheless," said Abby, "it is my fault he's in trouble, and I will try to save him."

"It's not only your fault." Cheeto stamped his front paw on the ground. "If I hadn't filled his head with ideas about dogs being the same as wolves, none of this would have happened."

"We will all go," said Spike.

Abby pleaded, "You'll only get hurt yourselves. Why risk your lives in a fight you can't win?"

"Because that's what friends do," answered Cheeto. "And friends wouldn't let you go fight those coyotes alone, either."

Abby smiled and licked the top of Cheeto's head.

"It's settled," Spike said. "These coyotes are skittish, so we'll try to sneak through the tall grass and then startle them. With a little luck, they will run away long enough for us to get Flea and retreat back to the woods where we can hide our tracks."

Cheeto looked at Abby. "Can you sneak? Spike and I are very good at it, but can you do it?"

"I am good at chase and tag, but I will try to sneak, too," said Abby.

At that, the three lowered onto their bellies and began to crawl through the grass toward the lone tree high on the hill.

"Help, help!" cried Flea Biscuit. "Wolf! Wolf! Help!"

"Cat!" hissed the lead coyote.

"Hungry!" said another.

The three rescuers quietly ascended the hill through the tall grass. As they approached the tree, Spike's fur began to tingle. He could see that Cheeto's orange stripes were puffed out, too, making him look much larger and more fierce.

The crawl had been most difficult for Abby, but she had struggled through it and not given away their presence. Now she was panting very hard, and drooling. All three were aware of how absurd it was for a dog and two cats to purposefully charge three wild coyotes, but they were committed to saving Flea Biscuit.

Chapter 11

Charge!

Suddenly Flea Biscuit let out a painful cry. One of the coyotes had jumped up and nipped him. He had almost been knocked off the tree! Now he was clinging to the branch by just a few front claws, struggling wildly to get back up. The three coyotes lined up beneath him licking their chops as if certain that they would finally have their meal.

Spike looked to his right at Cheeto and then to his left at Abby. She nodded. It was now or never. The three charged out of the grass, howling.

Startled by this sudden attack and confused by the sounds, the coyotes instinctively ducked into the tall grass and fled across the field. At that moment, Flea Biscuit's claws let go of the branch. He closed his eyes as he fell, certain he was about to be eaten. He landed and lay still. After a few seconds of silence, he opened his eyes. Instead of looking up into the snarling faces of three hungry coyotes, he saw his two friends looking down at him.

"Wow, am I glad to see you," he said weakly. He looked at Cheeto. "Where did you come from? Why are you here with that wolf?"

"She's not a wolf," Cheeto responded, embarrassed at how foolish he had been. "She is a dog and her name is Abby."

"She's a friend," said Spike, as he quickly looked left and right. "Now let's go. We haven't much time."

Flea Biscuit struggled to stand up. He looked at Abby. "My name is Flea Biscuit," he said.

Abby looked down at the little tiger cat and replied, "Well, I don't like fleas. I do really like biscuits, though, so I think we will be friends."

"Can you walk?" asked Cheeto.

"My leg hurts from the bite, but I will try."

Already the coyotes had stopped to regroup at the bottom of the hill. They were confused, but as they came back to their senses, they realized they had been tricked out of their meal. Abruptly they turned and headed back toward the tree. With each step, their pace quickened. Faster and faster they ran.

Spike was the first to realize the danger approaching. "We can't walk out of here," he yelled. "We need to run!"

Abby quickly lay down and in a calm voice told Flea Biscuit, "Get on my back and hold on! I will carry you home."

Flea Biscuit was still frightened of Abby, but Cheeto nodded for him to do as she said, so he climbed on. The four friends sped low across the field to the safety of the woods on the other side.

By the time the coyotes reached the tree at the top of the hill, no one was there. They looked at each other confused and unsure as to who or what it was that had surprised them.

"Gone," hissed one. They began to nip at each other in anger. The leader growled and looked about hungrily, then led them off toward the woods.

Chapter 12

A Night at the Lake

Flea Biscuit clung to Abby's fur as the group trudged through the forest. "How did you know where I was?" he asked. "Even I couldn't have found me."

"We had some help," said Spike.

"And a lot of luck," added Cheeto.

"It helps to have a dog's nose too!" said Abby as she sniffed the air, still checking for the scent of coyote.

They had been on their feet all day, and still had to retrace their steps back to the big old house. The journey would not be quick and the late afternoon heat was beginning to wear on all of them.

As they approached the lake they'd passed earlier, Abby stopped and said, "I need a drink of water."

"Agreed," said Cheeto.

From the front of the line, Spike added, "We'll stop to rest here. We're all very tired and there are shade trees by the water where we can climb and sleep safely."

Cheeto added, "We'll take turns keeping watch from high in the branches."

Abby knelt, and Flea Biscuit slid slowly to the ground. He looked around and saw the sun setting over the lake. Abby sprinted to the water and jumped in. The wave splashed up and over Spike and Cheeto, who ran away from it. "Be careful!" hissed Spike. Abby laughed and played in the water, finally cooling off after a long, hot day.

"Drink some water, house cat," ordered Spike. He and Cheeto approached the edge of the water away from Abby's splashing.

Flea Biscuit joined them. "Are we far from the house?" he asked.

"Aye, but we will be home tomorrow, little one," said Cheeto. "Now don't you worry at all. I will go and find us something to eat. There are many things we can eat in the forest, and I am hungry."

Spike jumped up on a large rock to survey the area just as Abby came out of the lake and began to shake the water from her fur. "Hey!" Flea Biscuit laughed as he jumped away.

Back and forth into the woods Cheeto ran. Each time, he returned with something they could eat. "He is a very good hunter," thought Flea Biscuit, until he looked down and saw the collection of insects, grubs, and worms that Cheeto had collected for them to eat. "Is this what stray cats eat all the time?" he thought. He did not want to eat these things. He was starting to back away when he saw the icy stare directed at him from Spike's piercing green eyes.

"Are you so delicate, housecat?" Spike asked in a superior tone. "If you were as hungry as those coyotes, you would be grateful to have such a feast."

Flea Biscuit resolved to be thankful for the food and to eat his first meal from the forest. He was very hungry and found that it did not taste as bad as it looked.

After eating the morsels Cheeto had caught, they thanked him and then rested by the water. The reflection of the moon shone brightly on the lake and lit the edge of the forest in a cool, friendly glow. Flea Biscuit heard a clicking sound and looked up to see something flap its wings and quickly pass overhead. "It's a flying mouse!" he said excitedly. "Can we catch one?"

"Aye, those aren't mice, little one. They are called bats and they are friends," answered Cheeto.

"I caught one in the house once," mused Spike. "The man was very careful not to cause any harm to her. He wrapped her up, carried her to the door, and let her fly free outside. The bat seemed very polite, and apologized for being in the man's home."

"Of course she was polite," said Abby. "She thought you were going to eat her."

Spike made a spitting motion and indignantly said, "I would never eat such a thing. I only caught her because she was in the man's house and that is my job."

Cheeto jumped up onto a branch of a tall pine tree. "Bed time, little tiger. We'll be safe up here."

Flea Biscuit struggled to reach the first branch, but soon was high enough to be out of danger from the coyotes, should they have been followed. "Good night, everyone," he said. "Thank you for rescuing me."

Spike took a deep breath of the night air, his sharp eyes surveying his surroundings. He loved being outside in the woods under the moonlight. It made him feel wild and young. He jumped up on the large rock again and looked out over the water as Abby curled up at the base of the tree. "Get some sleep," he said. "I'll keep watch."

Chapter 13

Homeward Bound

In the morning, after sniffing around, Abby thought she had found the direction they had come from. "Still," she said, "the trail is faint."

"If we can locate the possum's den, I'm sure he'll be able to help," said Spike.

"What do you think, Abby?" asked Cheeto. "Can you can lead us to Spike's friend?"

"Oh yes," said Abby. "I am very good at tag and chase and I got to smell him yesterday. He has a wonderful scent and will be very easy to find."

"Good," said Spike. "Lead on."

Abby knelt down to let Flea Biscuit climb on her back.

"Who is Spike's friend that we're going to see?" he asked.

"A wild creature of the forest," Abby replied. "Climb aboard and let's hope they are right and he can show us the way home."

After a short walk, they located the spot where the old possum made his home. "See if he's down there," said Spike.

Cheeto had barely started to poke his head inside the den when the grey possum came out nose-to-nose with him. "He's home!" laughed Cheeto.

"Oh, he can't help us. We're doomed!" wailed Flea Biscuit. "I asked him for directions before and he just stared at me."

Cheeto shook his head. "You need to show patience and kindness to creatures of the forest, Laddie. This possum knows many things, but he speaks the tongue of the wilderness and it takes time for him to understand us."

Abby lay down and Flea Biscuit slid off her back to stretch his three good legs. Then he sat down and licked his injured paw.

"Does it hurt?" asked Abby.

"Not much. It was not a very strong bite."

"Aye," joked Cheeto. "Perhaps they didn't like the taste of you after all?"

Flea Biscuit giggled. It was good to be here with his friends again, he thought. Even his new friend, Abby.

Spike conferred with the possum, and then they all sat patiently and waited. Just when Flea Biscuit was about to comment again on how pointless this was, the possum raised his head and stretched his paw toward a nearly hidden path.

"Home is this way," said Spike as he began walking toward the trail.

Flea Biscuit was confused. "How does he know the way to the house? I don't understand. Why are we following his directions?"

Spike turned to Flea Biscuit and commanded, "Quiet, Flea! There are ways of the forest that a child's pet like yourself will never understand."

Although he was hurt by how unkindly Spike had spoken to him, Flea Biscuit was sorry for misjudging the possum. "Thank you for helping us and being our friend," he said, although he doubted that the possum had understood.

In a kind voice, Abby turned and said to Flea Biscuit, "All aboard, little tiger. Next stop, home."

Chapter 14

Home Sweet Home

The sun was high and hot over the old house as the man and the farmer came wearily out of the woods. They were worried and discouraged after hours of searching for their pets. However, as they approached the home, they were astounded to see three cats and a dog all sleeping together on the front porch.

Abby was the first to awaken. She immediately ran to her master and jumped up to lick his face.

Spike watched from his spot on the porch swing and simply muttered, "So undignified."

"Oh, I don't know, Spike," said Cheeto from beneath the swing. "A little joy in your step might do you some good."

Flea Biscuit laughed as he walked toward the man.

Cheeto noticed that he wasn't limping at all. "Aye, little one," he called. "It seems your wound was not so bad!"

"Yes," said Flea Biscuit. "I would have said something earlier, but I was having so much fun riding on Abby."

"You little wildcat!" laughed Cheeto.

Spike rolled his eyes and laid his head back down.

Flea Biscuit giggled as the man scooped him up and carried him into the house.

Abby gave a quick wave goodbye, then she and her master walked back toward their farm.

"Well, Spike, how about some dinner?" asked Cheeto. "We've earned it, and I'm certainly hungry."

Spike stood and began to stretch. "You're always hungry," he said.

Chapter 15

A Fortunate Cat

The next few days were filled with fun as Cheeto and Flea Biscuit explored the big old house, played with toys, and most of all, took long naps. One morning, Abby was allowed to come into the house for a visit. She did not chase after Flea Biscuit this time, but instead let him take a nap with her. For the most part, Spike kept to himself while the others had their fun.

Then, late one afternoon, a car pulled up. Out hopped the little girl, followed by her mother. The little girl ran toward the house.

Hearing the car doors close, Flea Biscuit jumped to the window and looked out. He turned to Cheeto and, with a hint of regret in his voice, gave his old friend the news. "My humans are here. It's time for me to go back to my home."

"Aye, laddie," nodded Cheeto, "but I hope to be seeing you again very soon."

"Me, too!" said Flea Biscuit. "What an adventure we had!" He looked around and then asked, "Where's Spike?"

Cheeto glanced from side to side, then bent low. "He's been rather grumpy ever since we got back from the forest," he whispered, "so I'm leaving him alone for now. I'll be sure to tell him you said goodbye."

"Yes, and please tell him thank you, again," said Flea Biscuit.

Footsteps came quickly down the hall, then suddenly Flea Biscuit was scooped up into the little girl's arms where he always felt safe and happy. He began to purr loudly, and she giggled and stroked his fur.

The man gave her mother a hug and then walked them both to the door. The little girl poured Flea Biscuit back into his carrier and closed the latch. He paced around in a circle a few times to find the right spot on his blanket, and then lay down to rest for the ride home. The little girl picked up the carrier and walked outside toward the car.

Peering through the grate in his carrier, Flea Biscuit could see the man talking to the woman on the porch. She leaned in and gave him a kiss! This confused Flea Biscuit greatly. Then he noticed Spike on the porch swing. He was watching the kiss as well and looked surprised. "Goodbye, Spike!" shouted Flea Biscuit. Spike nodded to him just as the little girl placed the carrier on the back seat of the car and closed the door.

Soon they were headed down the road. "It has been quite a summer vacation," thought Flea Biscuit. "I saw old friends, made new ones, and learned many important things. Now I get to go back to my very own home. I am a fortunate cat." He laid his head down on the blanket and went to sleep.

Chapter 16

Star-Spangled Banter

Cheeto was cowering under the couch. There were strange flashes in the evening sky, and the sounds of thunder, but no rain. Spike had gone upstairs to investigate, but the orange tabby had decided to wait it out. When Spike didn't return, he began to get curious. Since it seemed there was no immediate danger, he crawled out to join his friend on top of the house. Quietly, he walked through the darkening rooms, up the stairs, down the hall, and then into the stairwell that led to the attic. After squeezing through the open attic window to the roof, he spotted Spike's dark frame silhouetted by flashes from the lights in the sky.

He crossed the roof and sat beside his friend. Above and below them, the bats were busy hunting for insects in the yard, but for now, the two cats ignored them. Instead, they gazed intently as rockets rose into the sky and burst into colorful showers of light and sparks. After a particularly loud explosion, Cheeto flinched.

"It's nothing to worry about," said Spike.

"Is it a storm?" asked Cheeto.

"I'm not sure," his friend replied, "but I've seen it before and it always stays far away."

The two cats sat on the roof admiring the colored lights. After a time, there was a tremendous build-up of explosions, and then, as quickly as it had begun, it was gone. The summer night showed no evidence of the display except a few twirls of smoke drifting a final waltz in the sky.

"I don't know what that was," said Cheeto, "but it was beautiful."

"Yes," murmured Spike. He sat nearly motionless, staring into the quiet night. Eventually the sounds of an owl hooting, bats clicking, and crickets chirping could be heard again.

"I wish Flea Biscuit had been here to see it," said Cheeto.

There was a long moment of silence until Spike at last responded with a quiet, "Yes."

Spike was lost in thought. He had discovered much about himself since Flea Biscuit had become lost in the woods. In spite of the risk and hardship, he had enjoyed the adventure of returning to the wild forest to rescue the little tiger. He had appreciated being part of a team, too, and was even more surprised to think that he had become friends with a dog. It troubled him that he had always thought poorly of dogs. Maybe he had even hated them, for no reason other than their being different. It made him feel ashamed. He also considered the plight of the coyotes. Although they were very dangerous, he felt pity for them.

"Will you be going down to hunt now?" asked Cheeto.

In a low, quiet voice, Spike answered, "No. I think I will stay up here for a while longer."

After a pause, Cheeto replied, "Then I will stay up here with you."

For most of the evening, they remained side-by-side, high on the rooftop of the big old house, looking out over the fireflies in the yard, beyond the tops of the trees, and into a sky filled with twinkling stars.

The End

Flea Biscuit's Summer Vacation

WRITE TO THE AUTHOR

Do you have a cat or other pet? I'd love to hear your story.

You can contact me or my cats at:

MBonazzoli@gmail.com.

Visit Flea Biscuit and Friends on the web at:

www.Fleabiscuit.com.

Made in the USA
Middletown, DE
24 November 2020